For Elsa, my heart
—ARS

For all children, you are beautiful. You are worth so much more than you think.
—ZC

· ·

Author's Note

This book is inspired by my three daughters. Like Elsie, one of my girls has Wolf-Hirschhorn syndrome (WHS), which affects 1 in 50,000 births. WHS is caused when part of a chromosome, a tiny building block of information in our bodies, is missing. Chromosomes determine all sorts of things, from our hair and eye color to how our bodies move and work.

People with WHS can have similar facial features and use many of the same tools to eat, move, and talk. In this story, when Elsie is hungry, her parents use a plastic tool to push a nutritious milkshake into her stomach. She also licks and tastes blended foods, such as applesauce, pudding, and icing. Elsie wears orthotics inside her shoes to make her ankles and feet strong. She can stand and take steps with help, and she also uses a wheelchair.

Some people with WHS talk verbally or use sign language. Others, like Elsie, use a book or tablet. Elsie talks with a PODD book, which stands for Pragmatic Organization Dynamic Display. She chooses her words by touching picture squares. Other PODD users choose words by shaking their head "yes" or "no" when they see or hear the word they want to use.

I hope that children who use PODD books and wheelchairs enjoy seeing a character with similar tools at the center of a story, and that children unfamiliar with her equipment like learning about it and getting to know Elsie.

· ·

Published by Two Lions, New York
www.apub.com

Amazon, the Amazon logo, and Two Lions are trademarks of Amazon.com, Inc., or its affiliates.

ISBN-13: 9781542007191
ISBN-10: 1542007194

The illustrations were created digitally. Book design by Tanya Ross-Hughes
Printed in China
First Edition
10 9 8 7 6 5 4 3 2 1

Dancing with Daddy

by Anitra Rowe Schulte

illustrated by Ziyue Chen

two lions

Elsie looked back and forth between two beautiful dresses.
Which one would Daddy like the best?
I'd look like a princess in pink . . .
But this one matches Daddy's soccer jersey . . .

Elsie grabbed the red dress and pulled it close.
This one. It's perfect for dancing with Daddy.

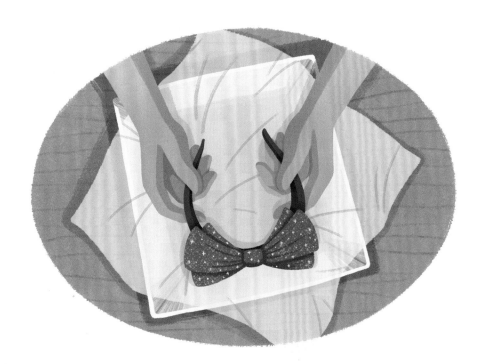

A clerk wrapped up the dress along with a matching bow.
The tissue paper crunched like fresh snow.

Mom drove home slowly.
As white flakes flurried,
Elsie worried.

*Will the dance
be canceled?
I hope the snow
stops soon . . .*

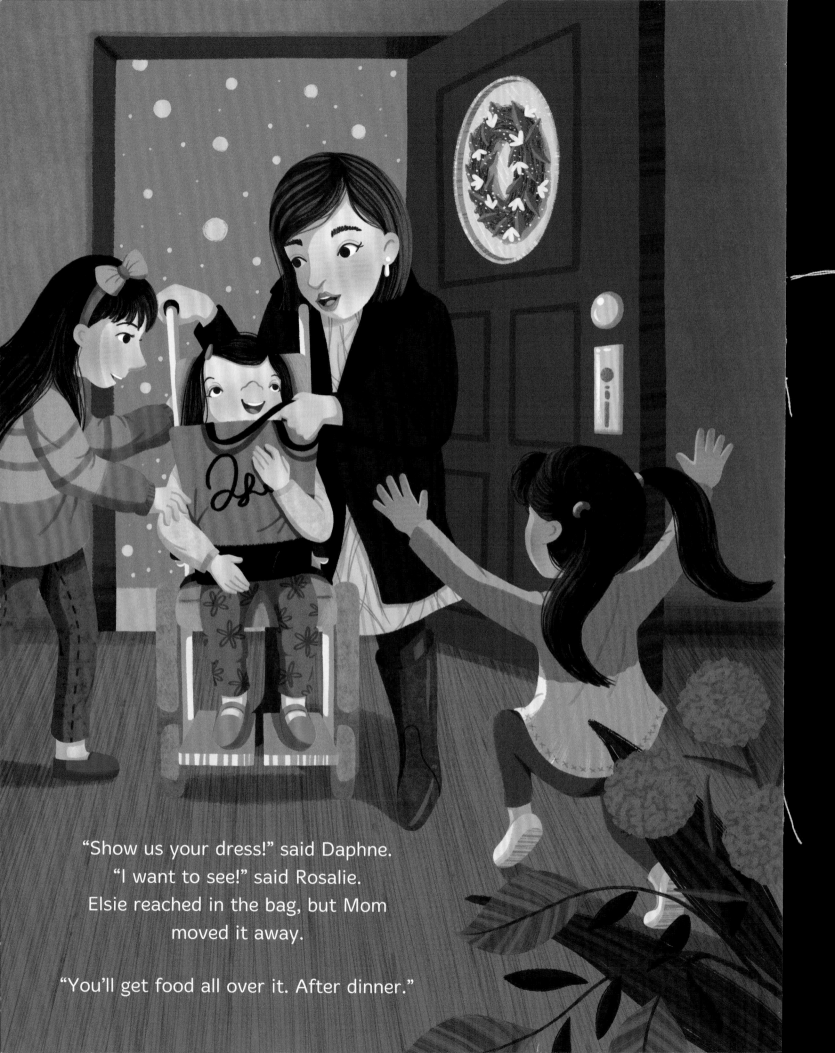

"Show us your dress!" said Daphne.
"I want to see!" said Rosalie.
Elsie reached in the bag, but Mom
moved it away.

"You'll get food all over it. After dinner."

"Hey, sweetheart," Daddy said. "Did you pick out a good one?"
Elsie pointed to *special* in her book.
"All right! Now you're ready to party with the big girls."

Daddy gave Elsie a push of food. It felt good in her belly.
Slippery noodles were hard to eat, but Elsie loved tasting sweets.
I bet they'll have cake at the dance. Yum, frosting!

After dinner, the girls hurried to see the dress.
"It reminds me of Daddy's jersey," said Rosalie.
"He'll love it," said Daphne.
Elsie beamed and blushed.

Knock, knock.

Daddy read Elsie's favorite bedtime book.

As the dancer in the story twirled, Elsie's heart did pirouettes.
I can't wait to see my dress spin.

That night, Elsie dreamed of dancing with Daddy.
And while she snoozed, it snowed . . .
and snowed . . . and snowed . . .

Elsie woke to the sound of
Daddy's shovel on the driveway.
The dance is canceled.
I just know it.

"Morning, love. I have some news . . ."

"The dance is a go!"
Elsie squealed with delight.
The girls practiced their dance moves all day.

Elsie swayed . . .
and twirled . . .

and dipped until she found
her groove.

Finally, it was time to get ready.

"You all look beautiful," said Daddy when they were ready.
"Great dress, Elsie!"

Thanks, it matches my . . .
Oh no! Where's my bow?
But it was time to go.
Daddy and the girls rushed out. The night was frigid,
but Elsie felt hot all over.

When they crossed the parking lot,
Elsie's wheels stuck in slush.
Daddy pushed
and pushed.

Inside, daughters dashed. Ponytails bounced. Dresses flounced.
Each dancer reminded Elsie of the girl in her favorite story.

The lobby was empty when they finally made it in.
Elsie's cold dress lay heavy on her lap.
She touched her hair where the bow should've been . . .

"Thanks for the reminder, honey," said Daddy.
"We can't go in without this."

He put the bow in place, then gave Elsie's chair a spin.
Her ruffles took flight.

Daddy opened the gym doors,
and music rushed out.
Elsie's heart thumped as
the bass boomed in her chest.

Under brilliant beams, the girls swayed . . . and twirled . . . and dipped.
After a flurry of fast songs, a slow and tender tune began to play.

"I need a break," said Daphne.
"Let's get punch," said Rosalie.

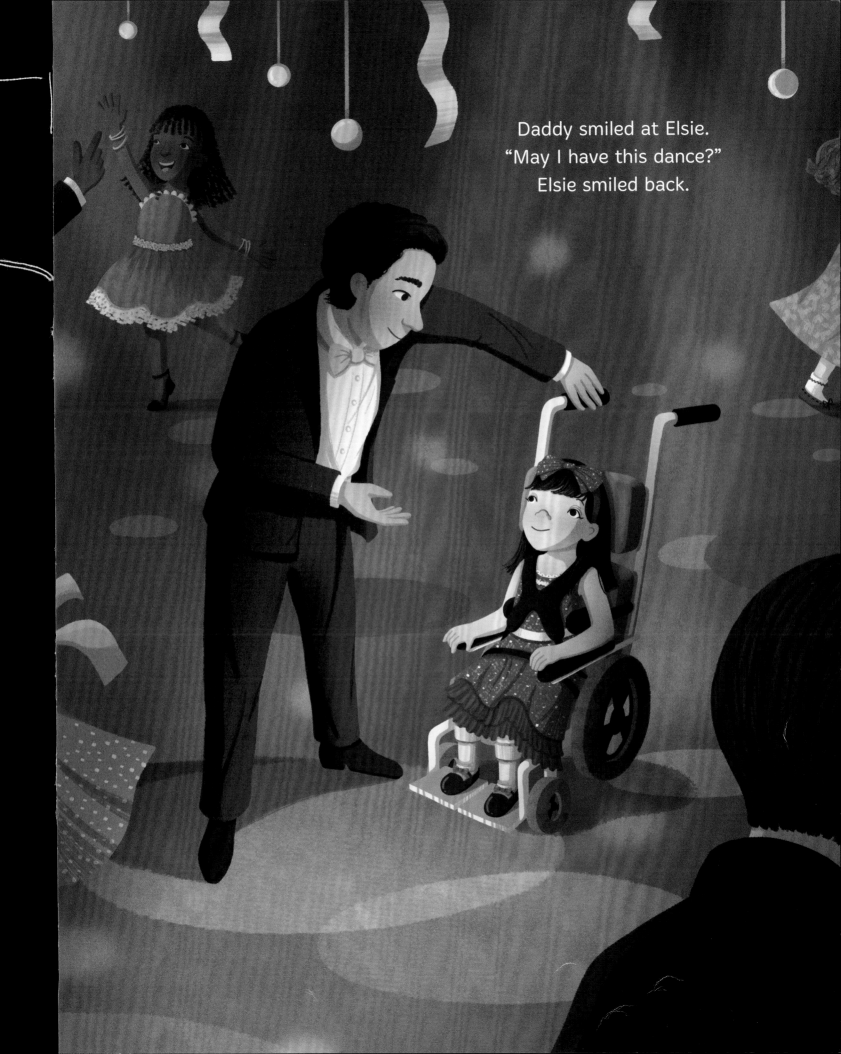

Daddy smiled at Elsie.
"May I have this dance?"
Elsie smiled back.

"Your dress reminds me of my jersey.
Except bright and beautiful.
Like you."

Elsie pressed her forehead against Daddy's,
and together they danced.

It was just like she had dreamed, except better.

When the song was over, it was time for some cake.
Mmm, so good!

Then Elsie reached for her book.

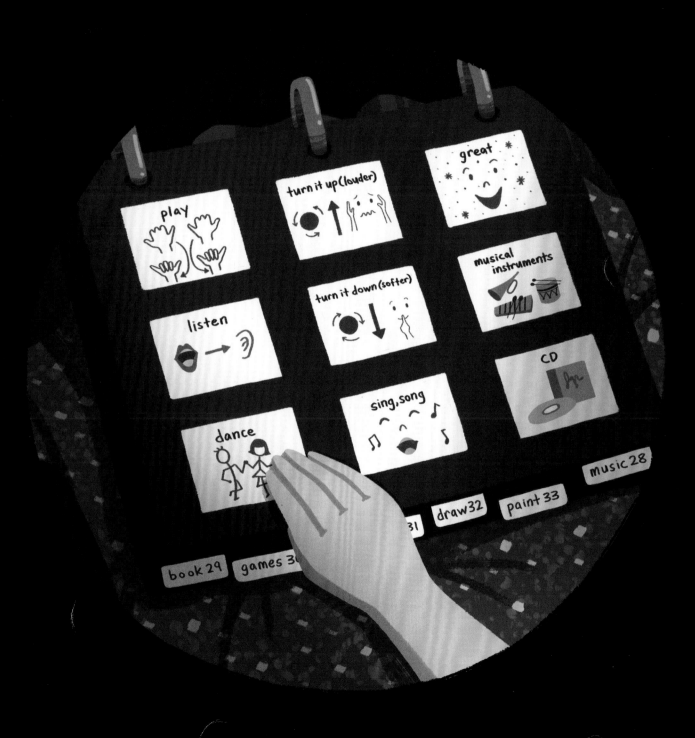

"You've got it, angel." Then they joined
Daphne and Rosalie under the lights
and danced and danced into the night.

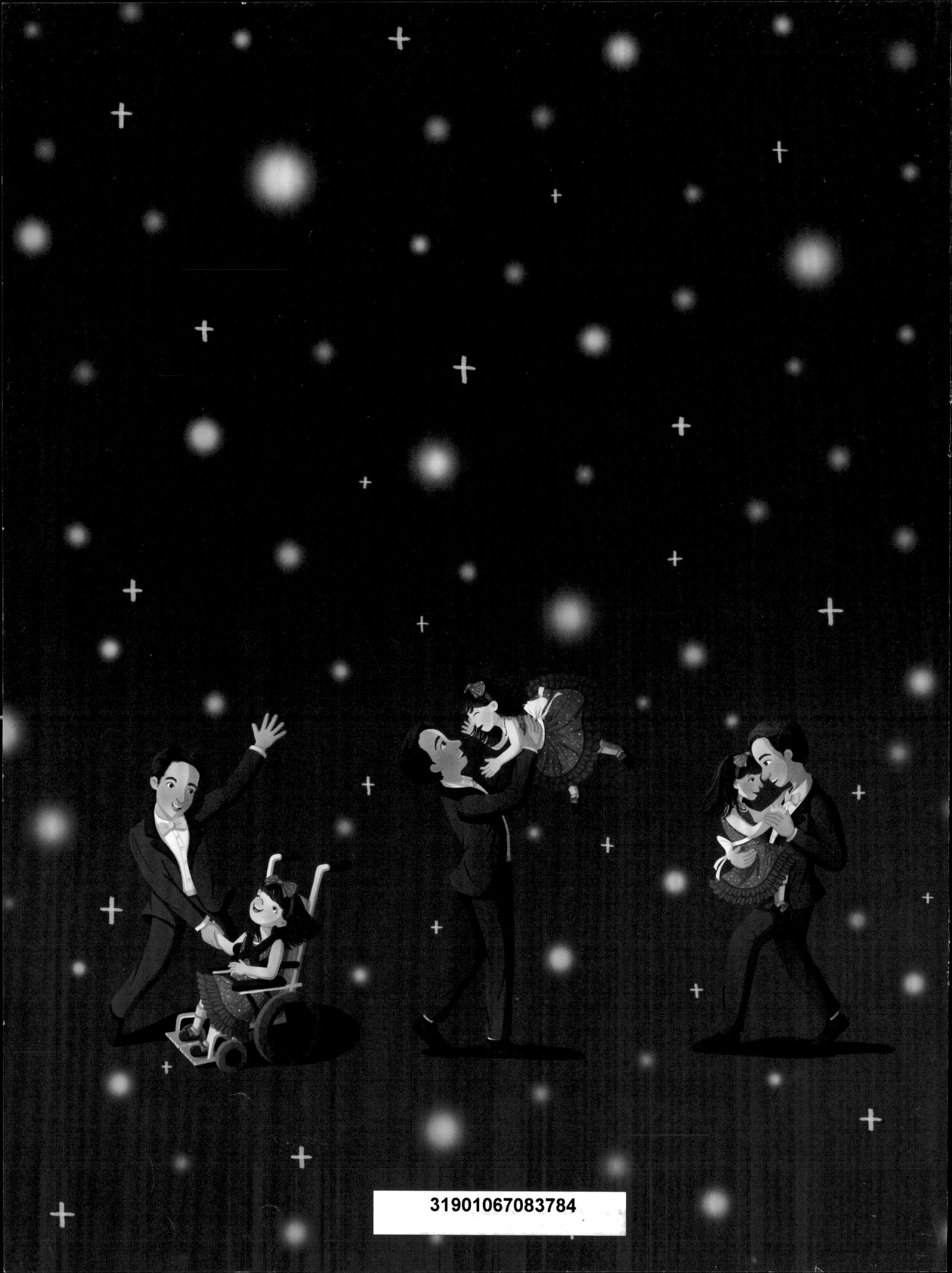